THE COW WHO FELL IN THE CANAL

THE COW WHO FELL
IN THE CANAL

by PHYLLIS KRASILOVSKY   illustrated by PETER SPIER

EGMONT

Hendrika was an unhappy cow. She lived on a farm in Holland, where it is very flat.

All summer long she ate grass.

All winter long she ate hay.

All winter and all summer she did nothing but eat.

And she gave milk to Mr. Hofstra, the farmer. Mr. Hofstra thought she was a fine cow because she gave such white creamy milk.

"Eat, eat, Hendrika," he would say. "The more you eat the more creamy white milk you can give me." Hendrika loved Mr. Hofstra, so she ate more to please him. But she was unhappy.

In front of the pasture was a road. Every day Pieter, the horse, came with a wagon to take Hendrika's milk to the city. Pieter told Hendrika about the city. "The streets are made of cobblestones and the houses have staircases on their roofs. People ride bicycles," he said.

Hendrika wanted to see the wonderful things Pieter talked about. She was tired of looking at Mr. Hofstra's house, the barn, and the windmill. The windmill wore a little porch. It went round and round in the wind.
It made Hendrika dizzy.

Behind the pasture there was a narrow canal. In the summertime a man came through the canal with a boat to take Mr. Hofstra's cheese to market. Hendrika liked the boats. She thought it would be nice to ride in a boat to market. Pieter said the cheese sellers wore coloured straw hats with ribbons. Hendrika thought a coloured hat would taste so good!

Poor unhappy Hendrika! She longed to see something besides the house, the barn and the windmill. Instead, she ate and ate and ate. And she grew fat, and then fatter, and then very very very fat. She grew so fat she could hardly move. She grew so fat she could hardly see!

One day she went farther and farther and farther along the pasture. She looked neither right nor left for she had eyes only for the sweet grass, and before she knew SHE FELL IN THE CANAL!

The canal was not deep but it was deep enough for Hendrika to get all wet.
She was too fat to climb out so she just stood in the water and ate the grass along
the bank. Mr. Hofstra didn't know that Hendrika was in the canal because he
was busy getting his cheese ready for market.

Hendrika was in the canal a long time. She ate so much grass that she became sleepy. But she couldn't sleep in the water. If only she could get back to the pasture! It was springtime and there were flowers to eat! She walked and walked along the edge of the canal eating grass when suddenly . . .

She came upon an old raft! She pushed and pushed, and finally she fell on the raft and it drifted away from the bank.

HENDRIKA WENT FLOATING DOWN THE CANAL!

Past the pasture went Hendrika. Past the barn, the house, and the windmill. Past the tulips. Past the neighbour's barn, house, and windmill. Past more tulips. Past another barn.

Another house. Another windmill. Still more tulips. And still another windmill.
Now Hendrika wasn't too sleepy to open her eyes.
There was so much to see on both sides of the canal!

A whole row of houses with stair-cased roofs passed by. Then some children on bicycles. "Look at the cow on the canal!" they cried, and followed after on the road above the canal.

Another row of stair-cased roofs passed by. Housewives were cleaning windows and scrubbing doorsteps. They laughed to see Hendrika floating along. They too followed along the banks laughing and exclaiming.

Soon a whole flock of people were running, walking, or riding along the bank following the raft in the canal.

Hendrika loved all the attention she was getting. She mooed with happiness.

Suddenly the raft stopped and two boys pulled Hendrika to shore with a rope. Hendrika broke away and ran down the street.

It was hard to run on the cobblestones but Hendrika was enjoying the city at last.

On and on through the streets she went, with all the people following her.

She looked into windows

and pranced into yards.

She sniffed the bicycles.

There was so much to see!

Just as Hendrika began to get a little tired she arrived at a big square.
Here were whole crowds of people.

Here were men wearing coloured straw hats with streamers. Here were balls of cheeses piled high.

The market was just as Pieter told her it would be.

And the green straw hat tasted just as good as she thought it would.

Mr. Hofstra was there selling cheeses, too. "Hendrika!" he cried when he saw her.
"I thought you were at home in the pasture eating grass, not here eating hats!
A hat is to wear."

He was so surprised. Everyone laughed at his bewilderment.

Mr. Hofstra pushed Hendrika into Pieter's wagon

and drove her home.

After that day Mr. Hofstra made certain that Hendrika was safe in the pasture. Hendrika didn't mind.

Now she had so much to think about as she chewed the grass, looking so pretty in a coloured straw hat with streamers!

For Bill who took
me to Holland

EGMONT
We bring stories to life

*Our story began over a century ago, when
seventeen-year-old Egmont Harald Petersen found a
coin in the street. He was on his way to buy a flyswatter,
a small hand-operated printing machine that he then set
up in his tiny apartment.*

*The coin brought him such good luck that today Egmont
has offices in over 30 countries around the world. And
that lucky coin is still kept at the company's head offices
in Denmark.*

First published in Great Britain in 1958
By World's Work Ltd
Published 1990 by Little Mammoth
Published in this edition 2012 by Egmont UK Limited
The Yellow Building, 1 Nicholas Road, London W11 4AN

Text copyright © Phyllis Krasilovsky 1957
Illustrations copyright © Peter Spier 1957

ISBN 978 1 4052 2409 3

A CIP catalogue record for this title
is available from The British Library